The Chocolate Cat

Written and illustrated by
De Pa

Special thanks to "Grampasgarden" for their support of
this project.

Additional titles from De Pa Publishing are available at
www.depapublishing.com

"The Cinnamon Bear"
"Abigail Plum and The Red Bandits"
"The Magic Window Box"
"Mirror Mountain"
"Abigail Plum and The Robot Regulators"

In a place of magic
and fairy dust
there once
lived a
chocolate
cat.

She was a
very beautiful cat,

but she was sad
because she was made
of real
chocolate!

So when her
friends played on
sunny days,

the chocolate cat just watched.

Her body was too soft to play.

On really hot days she would lay in a stream even though she did not like it.

One very hot summer day the chocolate cat found a cool cave.

"Oh,
I wish
I was a real cat !"
She sighed.

This cave was the home of a crystal cave fairy.

"How do I know you can do real magic?" Asked the chocolate cat.

The crystal cave fairy waved her magic wand and the cave was filled with magic.

"Yes, but my magic is not free!"
The crystal cave fairy said.

Around and around the fairy flew yelling at the chocolate cat. "You must pay for my magic."

This made the chocolate cat very angry and she pounced on the fairy.

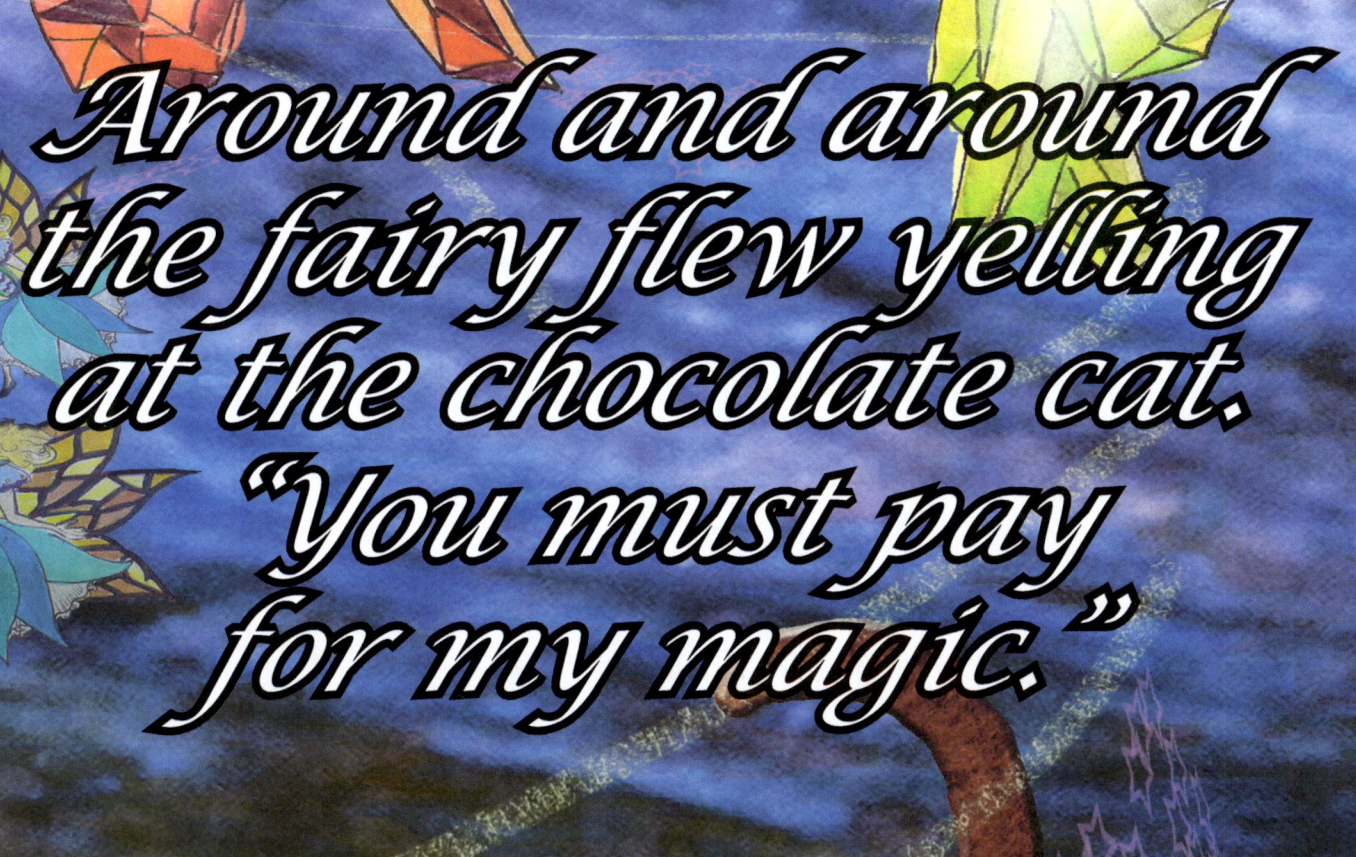

or I will bite you!"
The cat warned.

Tired of the foolish cat, the crystal cave fairy bit her paw.

"You bit me," the cat said sadly.

"Mmmm," said the fairy.

The Chocolate cat
liked that idea so
they did!

Later the crystal cave fairy invited a few friends over for a yummie chocolate snack,

and happily the chocolate cat went to find her friends.

The End

www.ingramcontent.com/pod-product-compliance
Lightning Source LLC
Chambersburg PA
CBHW041007170626
46815CB00002B/192